BALI RAI

DREAM ON

D1149561
9030 00004 1007 1

To Liverpool FC – the team that made me
fall in love with football.

And in memory of the 96 who lost their lives at
Hillsborough on 15th April 1989.

You'll never walk alone.

First published in 2002 in Great Britain by
Barrington Stoke Ltd
18 Walker Street, Edinburgh, EH3 7LP

www.barringtonstoke.co.uk

This edition first published 2014

Text © 2002 Bali Rai

The moral right of Bali Rai to be identified as the author
of this work has been asserted in accordance with the
Copyright, Designs and Patents Act 1988

All rights reserved. No part of this publication may be
reproduced in whole or in part, in any form without
the written permission of the publisher

A CIP catalogue record for this book is available
from the British Library upon request

ISBN: 978-1-78112-422-2

Printed in China by Leo

LONDON BOROUGH OF WANDSWORTH	
9030 00004 1067 1	
Askews & Holts	15-Jan-2015
JF TEENAGE 11-14	£6.99
	WW14002428

CONTENTS

1. Fish and Chips   1

2. A Chance?   9

3. Mandip's Plan   19

4. The Plan in Action   28

5. The Trial   37

6. Hannah   47

7. Result!   57

1. FISH AND CHIPS

"Do I have to work in the shop today?" I asked my dad.

I hated working in our fish and chip shop. It was boring and smelly. And greasy too. Loads of kids from my school came in and all I ever heard from them was, "Chips an' curry sauce, mate!"

When I was younger, it was quite funny, being asked for that all the time. But after a while, it just got on my nerves. It wasn't strictly a fish and chip shop either. My old man sold Indian-style food too – samosas and pakora and kebabs, and curries of course. For years, I thought he had the only chippy in England that was really an Indian takeaway in disguise. Until one of my uncles opened one in Birmingham.

"This is how we making our money, beteh," my old man would say to me in his own peculiar brand of English. "Those trainers you wearing were paid for by fish an' chips."

"Yeah, I know that, Dad, but I wanna go out with me mates."

"Out? Out where? I paying you money to work and do your duty to the family. I make sure that you finish your homework, and all you want is to go out. Tell me, do your friends pay you to go out? Eh?"

"Don't be silly, Dad. And anyway, I need a life outside of this place. Otherwise how am I supposed to grow up like a normal person? I'll probably turn into a battered fish before I escape from here."

My dad looked at me like I was proper crazy.

"Now who is being stupid? If you want outside life, how about school?"

"Ah, you ain't even listening, Dad. What's the point of talking to you?"

"I am listening, Baljit. Now pass me that bucket of chips and go and get some frozen samosas from your mother." Dismissed. Just like that.

I went over to the big yellow bucket into which I had thrown what felt like a million chipped potatoes earlier, and I dragged it over to my dad. I wasn't going to pick it up. Raw chips weigh a ton. Over the counter, I saw our first customer come in. It was Mr Biggs, a pensioner who lived up the street.

I knew it would be Mr Biggs. He was always our first customer. He always wore his old brown leather shoes, and the same pair of faded brown pinstripe trousers with brown braces, and a cream-coloured shirt tucked in. This was finished off with a grey overcoat and a grey felt hat, which Mr Biggs told me was called a fedora.

I felt sorry for him. I remember when his wife died, when I was younger, and for about two months he didn't come into the shop. My old man was worried about him and asked all our neighbours if they had seen him. No one had. And then one day he was back, only he looked older and frailer, and he smelled kind of musty.

Since then, my dad only charges him for his chips on Monday, though he comes in every day. Monday's when he gets his pension. Dad thinks giving Mr Biggs free meals is a way of doing his duty as a Sikh. Part of the Sikh religion is to provide a free kitchen to those less fortunate than you, no matter what colour or religion they are. It's called the "langar". My old man provides it for Mr Biggs and another pensioner, Mrs Benjamin, who's from Jamaica. But no one else.

"Be out of the business if I did," he always tells me.

Mr Biggs waited, like he did every day, for the first batch of chips to come out of the fryer, and he moaned to my dad about how the area we lived in seemed to have changed for the worse.

There was rubbish on the streets, he said, and cracks in the pavement and the council just didn't care. What if he caught his toe on a crack and broke his neck falling over? Who'd look after his poor wife, Elsie, then? Heh?

Then my old man reminded him that Elsie was dead. Mr Biggs nodded and looked kind of sad. They spoke some more and then Mr Biggs ordered his chips. "None of that curry sauce, mind. That's for you rag heads. I'll have a little tub of gravy, Mr Sandhu."

My old man laughed at the way Mr Biggs called us rag heads. I didn't think it was funny, joking about turbans. But my old man told me that old dogs can't be taught new tricks, only he had a Punjabi version, which involved a long story about a lazy old water buffalo and a young herder with a big stick. He told me that Mr Biggs wasn't really a racist – he just didn't know there were some things you just didn't say.

"I would rather he calling me the rag head than smashing up my shop, beteh."

By which I think he meant that it's not words that can hurt you.

He gave Mr Biggs his food and said, "No money, please," like he always did.

"Ay, you're a good 'un. I'll have to get you a good bottle of whisky one day, Mr Sandhu." This was Mr Biggs's usual reply.

Then he turned to me and smiled. "All right, kid? How's the footy going?"

"It would be good if the old man let me out of here for once," I replied, ducking as Dad threw a greasy chip at me.

"Make a lot of money playin' football these days," Mr Biggs said. And then he turned and walked to the door still talking. God knows who he was talking to. "Ah, course, in my day ..." he was saying.

I worked in the chip shop almost every night. But first, I'd get home from school, eat and then do two hours of homework or reading. I had to. My old man made me.

"Knowledge is power, Baljit." He believed that education would make me a better man. That and getting sweaty and smelly in a chippy.

And I wished he'd call me Jit for short. I hated my full name. But my old man would rather not speak to me at all than call me by the name all my friends used.

I'd enjoyed working in the chippy as a kid. It was like a great big adventure and my dad was the action hero. I remember seeing blokes coming in all tanked up, calling my dad all kinds of racist names, and he would just smile and take their money.

If they got really nasty he'd tell them to "leaving my shop you". Or sometimes he'd go bright red, grab the big old kebab knife from under the steel counter and go through the hatch, into the shop.

My dad is a big man and not one of those hard blokes stood their ground when he went mad. They just left, scattering their chips on the floor, curry sauce an' all.

It was when I started playing footy that working in the shop got annoying. I only had two days when Dad allowed me to play. There was after-school practice on Wednesday nights and then playing for the school team on Saturday mornings, but nothing more than that.

My two best mates, Danny and Mo, played with me for the school team. They also played Sunday League games for a local side which had really good links with the talent scouts from major clubs like Leicester City and Aston Villa. They went to more practice sessions than me and played more games. I wanted to do that too.

But my old man just told me I was stupid. "You playing one night in week and Saturday morning. That is enough, son."

"But, Dad, I wanna play more – like Mo and Danny. It's not like I'm out stealing cars and taking drugs every night! I just wanna play football."

"And I just want pay the bills, innit?"

"But how am I supposed to improve? You wouldn't complain if I ended up signing for Liverpool, would you?"

"How many Indian playing the football, beteh? They don't let us into the teams, innit."

"Only because people like you stop people like me havin' a go!" I was getting angry.

"Chadd deh, Baljit," Dad said, which means "leave it". And then he threw another chip at me. It was covered in batter and hit me in the middle of my forehead. The batter dripped down my face. Well, after that, how could I not start laughing and throw one back at him?

2. A CHANCE?

It was Danny and Mo that told me about the trials at Leicester City. Our school coach, Mr Ball, was also a youth team coach for Leicester. He looked after the under-14s team.

One of his jobs was to go around to different schools and look for talented players. He had mentioned an open trial for under-16s and told Mo that he thought all three of us would have a great chance of being picked for the team. When they told me, I got really excited.

Ever since I started playing football, I've always had this dream about becoming a professional footballer. About playing for Liverpool. I've loved them since I was a kid.

But as soon as I started dreaming about the future, I remembered my old man. There was no way he'd let me be a professional footballer. He wanted me to become a lawyer or a doctor. "These are the good jobs, Baljit. Never mind

the football. If you dream it must be for real.
Why can't you dream about things that really
matter?" That was his usual reply.

I was going to have to do something to
convince him I was serious.

I suppose I'd better tell you a bit more about my
two best mates. Danny is my oldest friend. We
have been at school together since we were five
years old. Danny looks like a 15-year-old Will
Smith – you know, the actor – and he's funny
like him too. He can find a joke for any moment,
although some of them are really bad. His
birthday is only one day after mine and we're so
close that we're like brothers.

Mo is Asian like me. His parents are from
Pakistan and he moved to our school when
he was 12. He used to live in Oldham, near
Manchester. That's why he's a Man United fan.
In fact, I'm quite surprised we get on so well, as
Man U are the sworn enemies of Liverpool. He
takes the mick out of me all the time because

his team wins everything and we've done quite badly recently. But that's all changing now. I keep telling Mo that his boys have had their time. Liverpool will soon be back where they belong. At the top.

Danny just laughs at us both. "I don't care who wins what," he always tells us. "I just wanna play for a Premier League team!"

Mo is a bit more serious than either me or Danny, especially when it comes to football. He likes to push himself and we call him the Motivator because he's always urging us on, telling us to run faster, try harder. It's like having a teacher as a mate. Strange. Mo's cool, though.

Danny and Mo told me about the trials after school. We were on our way home through some playing fields. They belonged to another school, our local rivals. The estate we lived on was on the other side of the fields. A narrow alley led from the last field into the shopping area where my dad's chippy was.

We were playing a dangerous game walking home that way. The kids from the other school would have jumped us if they had seen us. But we were too busy talking about the trials to be bothered.

"He ain't gonna let me go," I told Danny and Mo, talking about my old man.

Danny looked at me like I was mad. "Course he is, bro. Like he's gonna stop you."

"Danny's right, you know," said Mo. "Like, if my dad thought I might make it into the Leicester team, he'd start dreaming about how much money he'd be able to send home to Pakistan – to buy more land that he don't even need."

Danny just grinned. "You ain't even got to the trial, Mo, and you're already dreaming about being the first Pakistani lad to play for MoneyBags United."

"You know what I mean," answered Mo. "My old man is sure that we're gonna get kicked out of this country. That's why he sends all his money back to Pakistan."

"It'll be your money not his, if you ever do make it," I said.

"Yeah and I ain't gonna to leave this country. This is my home. Think I'm gonna play international games for Pakistan? Forget that, bruv!"

"Hey, day dreamer, there you go again. No one ain't asked you to play for England Ladies yet – never mind anyone else!" Danny was grinning again.

"Least I'd play the ladies," replied Mo. "You'd be too busy tryin' to get in their shorts."

"Ain't nothing wrong with that," Danny replied. "A healthy thing for any young man to do," he added in a daft BBC voice.

Mo scowled. "Why does every serious conversation we have end up being about girls?"

"Because you is too serious an' the ladies be what life is all about," said Danny.

"Your life, maybe."

I listened as Mo and Danny had a go at each other, but I was more interested in the trials. I wanted more details.

"So when is the first session?" I asked, trying to change the subject.

"Next week. Mr Ball is gonna drive us to it. It's at the training ground," replied Mo.

"What? The Leicester City training ground?"

"Yeah."

"Wow!" A trial at a Premiership club. Now I was excited. I was going and that was that. My old man would just have to lump it.

But then we heard shouting behind us. I turned and saw about eight lads from our rival school running towards us. They looked bigger and older than us.

Danny saw them too. "Hey you two, forget your serious chat and run!" he shouted and took off. I followed him.

Mo turned and saw the gang of lads. "Oh bollocks!" he said as he swung his bag on his shoulder and set off behind us.

We sprinted for the alley that led into the shopping precinct. It was about the length of a football pitch away and we were running like hell. I felt something whizz past my ear. It was half a brick. These lads weren't messing about.

As I ran, I was trying to work out what we had done to make them attack us. And then I heard one of them shouting racist abuse at us. The usual nasty rubbish like "Paki" and stuff. They were gaining on us, too.

Danny got to the alley first, with me right behind him. I turned to see if Mo was OK, just as he slipped and fell forwards, grazing his face on the gravel.

I stopped and ran back to him. He was shaking. I helped him up. The gang, who were all white lads, were about 50 metres away. I was bricking myself. "Mo, come on! COME ON!"

We set off again as more stones – smaller this time – flew past us. One of them caught me behind the ear. It stung, but I ignored it. I didn't know what we'd done to our attackers, but I wasn't going to stop and ask them. I don't mind getting into a fight if the odds are fair. Eight lads against three, though. Forget that!

As Mo and I ran towards the shops, I saw that Danny had reached my old man's takeaway.

He was coming out, my dad behind him, sleeves rolled up and my mum's chapati rolling pin in his hand.

My dad told us to wait in the shop. Mo went in, but Danny and I didn't want to miss the action. Dad headed for the alley to confront the gang and I wasn't going to let him go alone. Nor was Danny. We went after him.

The gang stopped as soon as they saw my old man. One of our neighbours, Mr Smith, who runs the barber's, came out and stood next to him. He was a retired policeman and he liked to think that the precinct was still his beat.

When the lads saw him too, they swore a few times, called us some more racist names and warned us to stay off their turf. Then, as my dad swore in Punjabi and shook the rolling pin at them, they ran away. The sight of him would have scared the hell out of anyone, I reckon. All of a sudden I was really proud of him.

Dad made sure that the gang had gone, then he came back to where Danny and me were standing with Mr Smith.

"Them effing kids," Mr Smith remarked. "I'd like to give their parents a piece of my ..."

"Parents more stupid than the kids, innit," replied my dad. "If my boy done that, I'd beat him me own self."

"Boy, that was scary," said Danny. He looked shaken but angry too. "See, when I catch them boys ..."

"They'll give you the kicking they couldn't give you today," I said, finishing his sentence.

"Them boys not worth the hassle, innit," my dad said. He walked off towards the barber's with Mr Smith, both of them moaning about how bad this country was getting. I turned and went back to our shop, hoping that Mo wasn't too badly hurt.

Mo was standing by the counter with a tissue pressed to his face. He had a few scratches, but nothing fatal. I took him into the back and cleaned his face up with a bit of cotton wool and warm water. Then he set off for home with Danny. Danny was still really angry, swearing and promising to take revenge. As he passed a rubbish bin, he kicked it over. I didn't say anything. Instead, when they'd gone, I picked up the mess he'd left behind and I thought about the football trials.

3. MANDIP'S PLAN

The following Saturday I got home from a match against another school to find that the shop was closed. It was just past one o'clock in the afternoon. Normally, my old man opened for about three hours over lunch on Saturday and Sunday to catch what he called "week ending trade". At first I thought that something was wrong, but when I walked into the house it was full of people.

My uncle Ranjit and his family had come to visit from Birmingham. Real Brummies, they were, with those proper thick accents. My uncle and aunt had just had a baby boy and they'd come over to celebrate, Punjabi style, which meant loads of food and booze and loud music.

My uncle had two older kids already – a lad called Jagdip and a girl called Mandip. Jagdip was ten and he did my head in. He asked questions every five seconds about anything and everything, and he never shut up. Mandip was my age, though, and she was great. She was wearing a traditional Punjabi outfit – a loose top and really baggy trousers, and I knew she hated it. She always complained about them.

"I feel like a clown, Jit. People just stare at me, innit?" Her complaints made me laugh every time. Partly because she did look like a clown, but mostly because of her accent.

My uncle was similar to my old man. Big and strong, and he liked to drink. He owned a car repair garage and was always going on about the last job he'd had or the latest Merc this or BMW that. But he was a good laugh. He was in the living room when I got in and he got up and gave me a bear hug that squeezed the air out of me. "Baljit, beteh. How are you? Working hard for your father, eh?"

My dad laughed at that. He pointed to the coffee table, which was loaded with food. Samosas and pakora and a plate of tandoori chicken as well as tea and glasses of mango juice.

"Eat something with us, Baljit. Your uncle has a new baby boy," he said, proudly.

My uncle nodded and slapped my shoulder. "You getting close to the age where you gonna be giving us grandkids soon, innit," he said, knowing that it would wind me up.

I shook my head at him. "Not before I become a footballer, Uncle-ji. Maybe after that."

My uncle laughed.

"Football – that all he care about," my dad said.

"And how that going?" My uncle asked the question, but he really wasn't that interested. He picked up a samosa and stuffed half of it into his mouth before I got a chance to reply.

"OK. My coach says I could become a pro – if he let me." I nodded at the old man.

"You forget about football, son. You wanna get a good trade like me and your dad. People always need good mechanic, and these whites always gonna buy the fish an' chips."

"I don't want to sell chips an' that. I wanna be a star."

"Well, when you make the first million, don't forget your poor uncle-ji." And then my uncle laughed again and started to talk to my old man about boring stuff.

I wondered whether it was a good time to bring up the football trials. Dad was in a good mood with all the food and the booze, but I decided against it. With my uncle there it would be like going up against two dads not one. Hardly the best odds for the game I wanted to play. Instead, I went up to my room to get changed. I stayed there for a bit, thinking. How was I going to convince my dad to let me go to the trials on Thursday evening?

My pest of a cousin came to the door and tried to get in, but I wasn't having it.

"What you doin' in there, bhai-ji," he asked me about ten times. "Bhai-ji" means brother and he had to call me that because I was older than him. He'd been brought up to show respect for his elders, like most Punjabi kids.

"I ain't doin' anything, Jagdip. Go away," I yelled through the door.

"You got a computer in there? Can I play on it?"

"Yes and no. I have got a computer, but you can't have a go on it. I ain't got no games anyway. I use it for my homework," I said.

"You're lyin' – I seen you playin' on it last time we come 'ere. Let me play." He just wouldn't stop whining, the annoying little git. Where was the respect now?

"Get lost, you brat!"

"I'm tellin' me dad."

"I don't care – I'm busy!"

I heard him walk off, and then his sister Mandip knocked in his place. I let her in because she was cool.

"Ain't you comin' down?" she asked, as she sat at my desk.

"Nah, Mandip. Can't be bothered. They bore me, talking about money and land all the time."

"Tell me about it." Her Brummie accent was so thick that I had to stop myself from mimicking her. She would have killed me if I had, and I'd probably deserve it, too. It wasn't like I'd never heard a Brummie speak before.

"Don't even wanna be 'ere. My friends was goin' up the Bull Ring and I wanted to go with 'em."

"But you had to come here instead, yeah? Family coming before friends, innit."

I was talking just like our fathers did, and we both laughed.

"Them two sound exactly the same, innit," Mandip said. "They're proper jokers."

"Tell me about it," I replied. "Does your dad ignore you, too?"

Mandip looked confused so I decided to explain.

"I wanna go to this football trial at Leicester City on Thursday. But my dad thinks footy is a waste of time."

"Leicester City? You mean the real thing?" she asked me, raising her eyebrows.

"Yeah."

"You that good?" She looked amazed.

"I dunno. That's what I was hoping to find out," I told her.

"Wow. Imagine if you got to play it for proper. All that money you could get."

"Don't think I ain't thought about it," I said.

"But I bet your dad wants you to work in the family business, yeah?" Mandip shook her head, like she'd heard it all before.

"Exactly. Or he wants me to become a lawyer or a doctor. Make him prouding."

Mandip laughed because I sounded exactly like the old man.

"You got to go then."

"How? I'm already playing on Wednesday night. He ain't gonna let me out Thursday. I'll be working in the shop."

"Just make up a story, Jit. That's what I do when I wanna go out."

It was my turn to be amazed. "What? I thought you was all shy and that?"

My cousin Mandip, the secret raver. How cool was that?

"It's all a blag, innit?" she said. "They think the same as you did – that I'm the quiet type, just into books and that. My local library don't close till eleven some nights," she said with a wink.

"I can't believe how sly you are," I said, impressed.

"You ain't a girl," she told me. "I got it harder than you."

I knew what she meant. Some Punjabi families are dead strict with girls. It was all about family honour and all that, and girls had less freedom than boys. I had to hand it to my cousin, though. She'd come up with a winning idea.

"So what excuse do I use?" I asked her.

"Someone's birthday?" she suggested. "A party?"

"Nah, they know when my best mates' birthdays are."

"School trip, then. Say you're going to London. Won't be back till late."

I thought about it for a bit. It would need a bit of work but it was good.

"Yeah, that's the one," I said. "Cheers, Mandip – you're a star. I owe you one."

"Forget it, Jit. Just buy me a car when you sign up for Liverpool." She smiled and stood up. "Come on, superstar, we'd best get back to the fun and games. They'll be asking where we got to."

I smiled and followed my cousin downstairs. "Sick trousers, Mandip. Where did you get them, off a clown?" I said, poking fun at her traditional Punjabi suit. Mandip scowled and poked me in the ribs.

"Keep that up and you won't be playing any football, ever," she said. I believed her too – she could be that scary!

4. THE PLAN IN ACTION

Later, I told Mo and Danny about the plan. They laughed at me to begin with, but then they saw that I was being serious and agreed to help. Danny told me that he'd print out a fake letter from the school for me. The fake school trip had just become "real".

Mo came back to the shop at about eight that night. He pretended that he'd been given the letter for me but had forgotten to hand it over. When my dad asked where we were going to visit, Mo, quick as usual, said the Science Museum and the British Library and my old man was really impressed.

"Good to learn things. Better than kicking the balls, innit."

Dad said the last bit so fast that it sounded like something else, and me and Mo cracked up with laughter. I was laughing at the way he'd fallen for our scam so easily too.

Dad must have been in a good mood because he told me that he was closing early. He asked me to write a sign for the window, to inform our customers. My uncle and his family were still with us, and my old man wanted to get drunk. When I asked him what to write he sighed and told me to "thinking you self". That made Mo laugh and then my dad threw a soggy chip at him, which hit his ear. At that I started laughing again.

"Telling you boys what." My dad was smiling and looking at Mo. "Today I not working. I celebrating Ranjit's new baby boy, innit."

"And?" I could sense something coming.

"How your friend like tenner to help you in shop tonight?"

I looked at Mo, whose face lit up at the mention of money. "Up to you, bro," I said, realising that we'd have a right good laugh in the shop together.

"Yeah, cool, Mr Sandhu." Mo grinned at my dad. Then he looked at me and winked.

"Right. That settle then," my dad said. "But you better ringing your dad and tell him you stay here, innit."

"He can use my phone, Dad," I offered. I wanted to call Danny over as well – make it a proper laugh.

"An' none of you messing 'bout, innit. This a business not a playground, OK?"

"Yes, Dad. Chill out," I said. "We're not going to burn the place down."

"Any mucking 'bout an' I killing the pair of you."

"Anything you say, Mr Sandhu," Mo said. "We'll be cool. And thanks for the tenner. I could do with the cash."

Mo was sucking up to my dad. Making out he could be trusted. He did it well too, because my old man shut up and left me to show Mo the basics. It was all pretty simple. How hard can frying a few chips be?

All through school the following week, I couldn't think of anything except the trials. I was so excited.

Danny was acting like he wasn't bothered, but I could tell that he was. He kept day-dreaming and in one lesson he called Mrs Turner, our English teacher, Mr Sutton – the name of our headmaster. That had all of us, including Mrs Turner, in stitches. But Danny couldn't even work out what all the fuss was about. He was on another planet – like something out of *Star Wars*.

When it got to Wednesday night and the practice session, all three of us were really up for it. We did about an hour of running and stretching and then played a 9-a-side game, with me and Danny on the same side, and Mo on the other.

It was really tiring but Mr Ball, our coach, told us to push harder. "Tomorrow is the big one, lads!" he said. "You'll be up against the best players in the county. So, if you want to get through, you need to put the hard work in. I believe in you – show me how good you can be!"

After practice, most of the other lads went home but Mr Ball kept me, Danny and Mo behind, along with a lad called Michael Beech who was coming to the trials too. He was a wicked defender but the main reason I liked him was his sister, Hannah, who was gorgeous.

I'd asked her out loads of times, but she was seeing this other lad and always said no. I was constantly asking Michael to put in a good word for me. In return, I offered not to make him look like a monkey on the pitch with my far superior skills. Funny enough, that didn't make him want to help me out.

We were sitting around in the changing rooms and Mr Ball was telling us what to expect when we got to the training ground. He went over the different skill tests we'd have to do.

The trial was going to be a 3-hour session and there was no guarantee that the four of us would be in the same groups. It was more likely that we would be split up and put with lads we didn't know.

I didn't mind. The way I saw it, if I was good enough I'd be able to play against anyone.

Mo was nervous, but for some reason I felt quite chilled out. I wasn't at the trials yet, though. I knew that, come the next day, I would be bricking it.

"Right then, lads. That's all I can tell you," Mr Ball said. "The rest is up to you. I wouldn't have selected any of you if I didn't think you could make it. Remember that."

"Thanks, Mr Ball," I said. His praise made me feel good.

"That's all right, Jit. I just want you to give it your all. Who knows, I might end up with a few Premiership stars on my hands!"

"You know it!" said Danny, grinning. "We are gonna kick some ass."

"Come now, Danny. Save all that for when you actually do get picked."

"Don't count them chickens, bro," said Mo, and he shook his head.

"Only chicken round here is you, mate," said Danny. "Specially with them legs."

"We'll see, bad boy."

Mr Ball cut in, before Danny and Mo went any further. "Right then, lads. I'll see you all after school tomorrow. Get some rest tonight."

With that, we made our way home, this time making sure we avoided the playing fields. It would be hard to impress at the trials if we'd just been beaten up.

My old man was in the shop and the smell of freshly fried chips was everywhere. I went to give him a hand, but it was really quiet. After about half an hour, I helped myself to a big portion of chips and some fried chicken and went to the back of the shop and up the stairs into the house.

My dad closed at about 10.30 p.m. and sat in the living room as my mum made him some tea. She brought it through and then sat down and asked me how school was going. I told her it was cool and then I asked her if she'd like to have a footballer for a son.

"You know your dad doesn't want that. Best you do well at school and not worry about all that," she said.

"But, Mum, what if I end up making millions? You and Dad wouldn't have to work in the shop any more. Look how tired you both get."

My mum smiled at me. "You're going to pay for us to retire?"

"Why not? What if I could?"

"You a funny boy sometimes, Baljit," she said. "Anyway, forget about football for just one minute and go to bed. You have school in the morning."

"Yeah, I've got that trip to London."

"Oh yes, your science trip. Do you need a packed lunch?"

I nearly choked. I'd forgotten about the minor details like a packed lunch. It was a good job that my natural talent for getting out of tight spots kicked in. "No, that's OK, Mum," I said. "You have enough to do. Can I just have some money so that I can buy lunch?"

Mum thought about it for a moment. "Yes, that's fine, but don't tell your dad. You know what he's like about wasting money." She looked over at my old man, but he had flaked out on the sofa.

"Don't I just." I smiled. "He's so tight you'd need a bomb to force his wallet open!"

Both of us started laughing at my joke, and that woke my dad up. "Hell you two laughing at? What you planning?"

"Nothing, Dad. Go back to sleep."

I didn't have to tell him. He was already snoring.

5. THE TRIAL

I got to the trial just before 5 p.m. About 30 lads were there, warming up on the pitch.

I was put in a group with some lads from three different schools around the city. One of them was a black lad called Tyrell Andrews. He played for the same Sunday League side as Danny and Mo and I knew him really well. He was Danny's cousin and played in the same position as me, central midfield. I think we were both pleased to see each other.

The pitch had been divided between four groups. Danny, Michael and Mo were in different groups – I could see them but I couldn't speak to them.

The coach, who was called Mr Jones, was giving us instructions about the tests we had to do. They involved dribbling the ball around flag posts, control skills, heading, passing and shooting at targets. We had to start with our weakest foot first, which for me was my left, and then do the whole lot again with the stronger foot.

I was doing OK, apart from when I lost my balance trying to turn and went flying into Tyrell. I was gutted, but Tyrell just helped me up. "Forget it, bro," he told me with a smile. "Just carry on as normal."

After 90 minutes of that, the entire group was split into two teams, and I got to be on the same team as Mo and Tyrell. The coaches started an 11-a-side game on the full size of the pitch. The players that were left out waited on the sidelines.

Every 10 or 15 minutes one of the lads playing was pulled off to allow another one on. I was waiting to go on, still trying to catch my breath after the last test. As I watched Danny tear our team's defence apart, I smiled. It was awesome to see my best mate doing so well.

Mo came off. "How's it going?" he asked and I told him I was fine but still bricking it a bit. He just shrugged and said that he'd had a nightmare. He'd been kicked on the ankle. It had swollen up so much that he couldn't play any more. He was gutted. Our school coach, Mr Ball, took him back into the changing rooms. I felt really bad for Mo but I didn't want to let his injury affect my own performance. I had a chance to shine and I was going to take it.

Blokes with clipboards were watching the game really closely and making notes about some of the lads. There were about 20 of them stood along both sides of the pitch, all wearing tracksuits. I wondered who they were. Leicester City wouldn't have that many youth team coaches.

When I looked back at the pitch, Danny let fly with a shot from about 20 metres out. It flew into the top corner and he turned and did a little war dance, a big grin all over his face. Then one of the other lads jogged off and I got a tap on my shoulder from one of the Leicester coaches.

"Baljit, your turn, son."

I jogged on and joined my team. Tyrell was already playing in my position, so I slotted in on his right. The other team had some big, strong players and as soon as I touched the ball, one of them took my legs out from behind me. I groaned as I went down and for a moment the wind was knocked out of me.

I lay on the ground, rolling around, thinking my trial was over already, but Tyrell and Danny came and helped me up.

Danny leaned towards me as the referee walked off, and he whispered in my ear. "You see that lad who just done you? Recognise him?"

I looked at the player who had fouled me.

"Last week, bro. The lads that chased us. He was the mouthy one."

"Yeah, now I remember. I'm gonna do him when he gets the ball." As I spoke, the lad mouthed the word "Paki" at me. Then he spat.

"Leave it, Jit. Not here. It ain't gonna help you get picked. We'll get him later."

The game restarted and Tyrell picked up the ball, twisted past a challenge and pushed the ball into space, wanting me to have a shot or play the strikers in.

As I gathered the ball, the racist lad tried to tackle me, holding onto my shirt. I put the ball through his legs and broke free, touched it past one of his team-mates and saw our striker run into space. I pushed the ball through to him and he placed it just past the keeper to make the score 1–1.

I didn't celebrate. I just shook Tyrell's hand and went back up the field for the restart.

About five minutes later, I picked the ball up in the midfield and passed it through the air, to the left winger. The ball landed right at his feet and I was well pleased. The winger took on his marker and then had to check back as there was no one in the box for him to pass to.

I sprinted into space, but he played it behind me. Tyrell got the ball instead and curled a shot past their keeper. It was a brilliant goal and this time half our team jumped him. We were in the lead. Yes! But as I made my way back to the centre circle the racist lad ran up to me and called me a "Paki" again and spat on the pitch right next to me.

This time I got properly mad and we got into a scuffle. The referee was straight over and told us both off.

"He just racially abused me," I told the ref, but he just shook his head.

"I ain't called him nothing!" the lad lied.

The ref shook his head.

"Cut it out – both of you!" he warned, before waving us away and the game kicked off again. My heart was going ten to the dozen and I was wound up like never before. I wanted to batter that racist loudmouth.

Tyrell shouted for me to move forward, which I did, as he brought the ball upfield. Again he skipped past two or three players like they weren't even there and then played the ball to me.

I had my back to the goal, and a defender right up behind me. I faked a turn to my right, which the defender followed, and then I went the other way. I was in space, with the goal 25 metres in front of me. I looked for a team-mate to pass to. There were two. Something made me ignore them. I wanted to prove that the racist lad hadn't beaten me. I wanted to show him that I was ten times the player that he was. So I just hit the ball.

The ball flew like an arrow, straight and rising. It smashed against the post and flew in. I couldn't believe it. I'd scored. I was on top of the world. My team-mates jumped all over me, and then it was back to the centre for the kick-off. This time the racist lad tripped me as I went past and called me some more names. Then he spat straight at me. He missed, but the ref saw everything and ran over.

"Right, lad, that's it. You're off!" the ref said, producing the red card this time.

"But ... he ..." began the lad, trying to play innocent.

"Racist and abusive language has no place on this pitch, son. You're off. And you can go straight home. You won't be asked back."

The lad went mental and told the ref to "eff off". His mates and his school coach had to drag him away. As I stood up, I heard the ref tell the coach that he would be reporting the school to the Football Association. The coach went red in the face and stormed off.

Ten minutes later, the final whistle blew and it was all over. I was knackered. My legs were shaking and my heart was pounding. Danny, Tyrell, Michael and me walked off together, all of us hyper and excited. Mr Ball told us how great we all were, even though Tyrell didn't play for him. I felt like I was flying – like I was unstoppable!

After we had showered and changed, we calmed down a bit, but were still talking about the trial. Mr Ball drove us home, dropping me and Michael off outside Mo's house before he took Danny and Tyrell back.

Mo was still gutted. The player who'd injured him was the same lad who'd abused me. I tried to tell Mo that we'd had the last laugh, but he didn't care. I could see his point, too. He hadn't had the chance to prove himself like I had. In the end I went home, hoping that Mo would feel better in the morning. I didn't think he would, though. I knew I wouldn't have.

I got in just after nine, walking through the chippy to get into the house, rather than using the side door. My dad was sitting behind the counter reading a newspaper. Or rather, looking at the pictures. I yawned at him as a way of saying hello.

"How was your trip, beteh?" he asked me.

"Cool. I'm really tired though."

"Is it raining outside?" Dad was staring at me.

"No, why?" I looked straight back at him.

"Because you have wet hair, Baljit."

Time for me to do a bit more of my famous quick thinking. "Yeah, some kids started a food fight on the back of the coach. They tipped a bottle of water over me."

I was well pleased with my quick-fire response, but my dad just shook his head. For a moment I was worried, but then he closed his paper, yawned and stood up.

"Telling you what. My day, teacher giving us slipper on back of head for that. World gone soft, Baljit. No wonder all them druggies all over the place."

"Yeah, yeah. I'd love to listen, Dad, but I've heard it all before and I just wanna eat and go to bed."

Thing is, I stood there for far too long. My mum walked into the shop and distracted me. I didn't see the sly grin on my dad's face. All I felt was his hand, covered in slimy batter, rubbing against my head.

"Dad!" I shouted, but he just grinned at me like a kid.

"Better getting in bath before bed, innit," he said, bursting into laughter along with my mum.

I just stood there as batter dripped down my face.

When my mum finally stopped laughing she told me to have a shower while she made me some food. And then she started laughing again till the tears rolled down her cheeks. Dissed by my own parents! Talk about being gutted.

6. HANNAH

"How do you think the trials went, then?" I asked Danny as we walked out of Burger King in the city centre.

It was two days after the session and at first I'd thought we'd been brilliant but had no idea if all those blokes with the clipboards had thought so too. Mr Ball wouldn't find out until the following week. But that didn't stop me itching to know.

"Dunno, bro," Danny said. "I reckon you and me done well. I mean, we both scored. What's better than that?"

Danny took a big bite of his cheeseburger as he waited for me to reply.

"It ain't just about that though, is it? They were looking for other stuff – like whether we can read the game and that."

"Reading? So you mean that whole thing on Thursday wasn't about playing footy? Like, were we supposed to read ...?"

"You fool. You know what I meant." I couldn't help laughing, though.

"Just gotta wait till Mr Ball gets the results. No use trying to make the future happen today."

"Why not, Mr Know-It-All?" I said, picking the gherkin from my cheeseburger and throwing it into a nearby bin.

"Er ... cos it wouldn't be the future then, would it?"

"Very funny."

We finished eating and walked into a sports shop. I was hoping to find a new pair of trainers in their sale. If my dad thought he was getting a bargain, he was more likely to give me the money. I swear, if there was a planet full of misers and they had a super-hero, it would be my dad. Captain Tight Wad, with his cash safely tucked away in his turban!

I had a good look around but didn't see anything that I liked. Danny got bored watching me pick up every pair of trainers and we went to play pool instead. Anything to get my mind off the trials.

We hadn't seen Mo since the trial. He'd skipped school the day after and texted me to say his ankle was really sore. I think he was feeling down too. I wanted to go and see him, but Danny said he needed some space. Like, to get his head sorted. Danny was right. I would have been the same as Mo, but I still wanted to make sure he was OK.

So, I waited until we'd finished playing pool and went to see Mo on my own. His house was only round the corner from mine, and I was hoping he'd cheered up a bit.

When I got to his, though, no one answered. I rang the bell again and again but it was no use. I gave up and headed home. I had to help Dad set up for the evening.

I spent the rest of the night peeling and chipping potatoes and frying them. The shop was very busy and old Mr Biggs, the nutter, came in as usual.

At about 9.30 p.m., I was behind the counter, wrapping cod and chips, when I saw Michael's sister, Hannah, come in. She was with her boyfriend but he looked really angry – like they'd been fighting. She walked up to the counter and smiled at me. "Hi, Jit."

I looked across at her and smiled weakly. I was going red. She was so fit. My old man saw my face and grinned.

"Not going to offer the young lady the reply, Baljit?" he said.

I could have killed him.

"That your real name? Baljit?" asked Hannah.

"Yeah." I watched as her boyfriend just stood there, looking angry and upset. She saw me watching her boyfriend and turned to him.

"You may as well go home, Joe. I'll ring my brother from here."

"But I can still walk you ..."

"No, you can't. I don't want you to." Hannah's voice was really stern, like a teacher telling off a pupil. "I don't wanna see you any more. I'll ring my brother to come get me and, anyway, Jit is one of my best mates. He'll look after me." She winked at me and I smiled back.

What a result! Hannah was splitting up with her boyfriend right in front of me. She was giving him the elbow in my dad's shop! And even though I felt sorry for Joe, I was still excited. Hannah was single. There had to be a god.

Joe stood and looked gutted for another five minutes before he finally pushed off. Hannah turned to me. "I've forgotten my mobile," she said with a grin. "Can I use yours?"

'Yeah," I replied, "but it's in the back. I'll have to get it."

My mum appeared behind me. She smiled and asked if Hannah was a friend of mine.

"Yeah, I'm his girlfriend," grinned Hannah.

I was that shocked you could have put a bucket of chips in my mouth. That's how wide it fell open. I didn't know what my mum would think about me having a girlfriend, especially one that wasn't Punjabi. What was Hannah playing at?

"Strange, he's never mentioned you before," replied my mum, giving me a funny look.

"She's messing about, Mum," I said, trying to cover my tracks.

"No she ain't," said my dad, butting in. "She very pretty girl an' all, innit."

I didn't know which way to turn. What was my old man up to? I was stunned. My mum was quite laid back, but I had always thought that my dad was proper traditional.

"I could really do with the loo, too," Hannah added.

"Well, don't keep her waiting, Baljit," said Mum. "Show her to the bathroom. And does she have a name?"

"Hannah," I said, helpfully. "I'll show her to the loo."

"Yes, Baljit, you do that. And then I think you and me should have a little chat."

Hannah followed me into the house as my old man grinned at me, taking the mick. When we were out of earshot, I turned to Hannah. "What was all that about?"

"What?" She shrugged and pretended to look confused.

"Since when were you my girlfriend?" I asked.

Hannah just smiled. "So you don't want to go out with me? Funny, that's not what Michael thinks."

"He ... he told you?" I was horrified.

"Told me? He tells me all the time. You keep asking him to." She smiled her cutest smile.

"What about Joe?" I asked.

"We've just finished. You saw it happen, Jit. I've been telling him for ages – he just didn't get the message." She stopped smiling and looked at me. Expecting something.

"So, are you asking me out or what?" she said, waiting.

"Er ... yeah. When would you ...?" I knew I was red like a beetroot but I didn't care. This felt even better than scoring that goal at the trials.

"Tomorrow night. We'll go to a film. Call for me at six."

Just like that. Like she had planned it all out before she got to the shop. Nimble as a ninja.

"Er ... cool." I had this strange feeling that I'd been targeted, surrounded and captured. Like some kind of army operation. And I had.

"Now, where's your loo?"

I looked at her and felt like I had to be dreaming.

"Don't worry about calling Michael," I said once my heart had stopped pounding. "I'll walk you home."

Hannah grinned. "That would be nice."

'You're telling me,' I thought, as I smiled inside and out.

When I got back in, Mum was waiting for me. She didn't look angry or anything. Just confused. My dad was closing up and I was in the back, with the sacks of potatoes and my mum, who was asking me a load of questions. Who was this girl?

Why hadn't I said anything about her before? How long had I been going out with her?

"You know, Baljit, your father and me don't mind if you go out with girls. We aren't like some parents. You were born in this country – you're bound to do what your friends do."

"I thought you'd be really angry," I said, not letting on that I had been tricked into going out with Hannah. Not that I minded. Not at all.

"Angry? Why would we be angry? Hannah seems like a nice girl. Do her parents mind that you are not white?"

"Nah, I doubt it. I've met them before. They're really cool. She's Michael's sister, Mum."

"Michael? Oh, that nice boy who comes in now and then."

"Yeah."

Then my dad walked in. As soon as he saw me he grinned again.

"Looking like you owe me one, innit. Fix you up with nice girl."

"I thought you wanted me to find a nice Asian girl," I said.

Dad laughed. "I wanting you to make something of yourself. Up to you about girls an' that, Baljit."

"You are full of surprises." I nodded at him and my mum.

"Bit like that girl, innit."

"Yeah, she sure took me by surprise, Dad."

I shot off into the house and rang Danny. I was well excited. I was going on a date with Hannah, Michael's super fit sister. Me. Every boy at our school fancied her. I was the man.

7. RESULT!

I was at school the following Tuesday, talking to Danny and Mo, telling them about my date with Hannah. Again.

Danny was trying to make out that we'd done more than just kiss, but we hadn't. We did snog loads but nothing else, and even if we had, I wasn't about to tell Danny. He was like a gossip site – one of those ones that spread nasty stories everywhere. He was always chatting. He pestered me all lunch time until I called him a "grass".

"I ain't no grass," he protested. "Don't be callin' me no rat. Never said anything to anyone."

If I hadn't known him as well as I did, I might have thought that he was upset, but he was only trying to pull my leg. I ignored him and asked Mo if his ankle was better.

"Yeah, the swelling's gone but I'm still angry. That lad tried to break my leg."

"I know. The ref sussed him, though. In the end." I was trying to make Mo feel better but it wasn't working.

"Well, I'm still gonna do him if I see him." Mo's face was set hard with anger.

"He ain't worth it, Mo," I warned him. "Let it go. There's bound to be another trial soon."

"Easy for you to say. You and Danny got to show what you could do."

I knew he was right. It was tough for Mo, but I didn't want to end up arguing about the trials. It wasn't worth falling out with my mate over football. And the mood Mo was in, I knew he'd lose his temper.

I saw Michael by the tennis courts and told Mo that I'd see him in English. I walked over to where Michael was standing with two of his mates.

"Thanks," I said to him. "For talking to Hannah."

Michael just grinned at me. "That's all right. She ain't stopped chatting about you," he told me.

"What, really?" I was chuffed.

"Yeah – must be love." He laughed.

"Don't be joking about your own sister," I replied, smiling.

"Forget about my sister for a minute, Romeo," said Michael. "Mr Ball told me that he knows about the trials."

"What? When?" Suddenly my attention shifted from Hannah to football. Just like that.

"This morning. He's gonna tell us just after lunch."

"I'd better go find Danny," I said. "Catch you later."

I found Danny by the main entrance. When he saw the look on my face he raised an eyebrow. "Don't tell me you've been snogging Hannah again?" he said.

"Nah. Just shut up and listen, Danny."

"Yes, boss." He laughed.

"Mr Ball knows about the trials, bro." I knew that would get him to stop clowning around.

"What?" Danny's eyes lit up.

"Yeah, Michael just told me. Ball's going to get us together after lunch."

"Nah! I can't wait!"

Twenty minutes later Mr Ball called us to an empty classroom. My heart was in my mouth. Mo was the only one that wasn't there. Danny was already talking about playing in the Premier League and what car he was going to drive. Honest, sometimes even I thought he was crazy.

Mr Ball was holding a letter for each of us and another that he had opened. "Well, lads. Let's see what we've got." He looked at Michael.

"Michael, you've been asked to attend a second trial at Leicester City next week. Congratulations."

Michael smiled from ear to ear and his face turned scarlet. He was well excited!

"Straight back to your classroom, son. I'll speak to you again tomorrow night."

Then Mr Ball turned to Danny. He told him that the blokes with the clipboards were coaches looking for new talent for their youth academies. One was even from Ajax, all the way from Amsterdam!

"Danny, you're going to be getting invitations from Leicester City, Coventry, Aston Villa and – I know this will make your head grow bigger than ever – Arsenal."

Danny just stood there. For once he had nothing to say. Not a word. I think he was in shock. I was. Arsenal – one of the best teams in Europe – and Danny was being offered a place at their academy.

Mr Ball handed him a letter. "That is an official invitation from Arsenal Football Club. Obviously, your parents need to know but well done, son. Fantastic news!"

Danny still hadn't said anything. He just stood there, blinking. At me. At Mr Ball. And then, slowly, his face lit up. When he smiled, it was dazzling.

"NO WAY!!!!!"

Mr Ball smiled back and Danny left for lessons. As he reached the door he shouted "Holy crap!" and gave a loud cry. Like an Apache warrior.

Mr Ball laughed and turned to me. I thought my heart was going to come flying out of the top of my head. But then what if I hadn't been picked by anyone? What if ...

"Jit, well, what can I say to you, son?" Mr Ball began, looking all stern. I thought I was going to get a telling-off. But then he smiled.

"You, young man, along with your friend Tyrell, must have gold in those feet of yours." He laughed again.

"What you on about, Mr Ball? Did we do OK?" I was getting nervous. I felt like I was going to be sick.

"You and Tyrell have been invited to second trials by every coach that attended, son."

I had to swallow hard. I nearly did throw up at that.

"But, two teams in particular want to see you both right away. Arsenal and Liverpool."

L-I-V-E-R-P-O-O-L. My team. My boys. I had to swallow again. My whole world went into a spin.

"Now, this envelope has your invitation letter in it. There will be more issues to sort out, but the youth coach at Liverpool is very, very keen to see you again."

"What ..." I couldn't speak, so I just shut up.

"I've been in touch with your parents and passed on the number of Liverpool's ..."

"Oh, hell!"

"What's the matter, Jit? I know it's a lot to take in."

"It's not that, Mr Ball. You don't understand. They don't know that I went to a trial – my parents – they don't know."

I was in trouble. Proper trouble. I had lied to them and now they'd found out. I told Mr Ball what had happened and all he did was smile.

Smile! There I was, about to get grounded for life for lying, and all Mr Ball could do was smile.

I trudged back to English, trying to find a way out of my problem, but all I could think of was how much grief I was in.

But after school, my troubles didn't seem that bad. All I could think of was L-I-V-E-R-P-O-O-L.

My feet didn't touch the ground on my way home. I decided it was better to tell the truth and face the consequences. After all, even though I'd lied, it had worked out well in the end. Liverpool FC – like, THE LFC – wanted to see me again. Surely even my parents wouldn't hold my lies against me after that?

But when I got in, all of that confidence disappeared. My mum gave me a stern look. "Baljit," she said. "Your father is upstairs waiting for you. I think you have something to tell us, son."

"Look, Mum, I only did it because ..."

"Go and talk to your father. I'm going to get some more chips cut and then I'll come up."

As I walked up the stairs, I thought, 'That's it, I'm done for.' I went to my room and dropped my bag and the letter on the bed. On my way to the living room, I prayed that my dad would be in a good mood.

As I walked through the door, my dad was waiting. He was holding a letter similar to the one Mr Ball had given me. I was about to start talking when he held up his hand. "Don't even start, Baljit. I have had a very strange letter today, from someone at Liverpool."

"Look, Dad, I can explain."

I was finished.

"So science trip mean playing the football, then?"

My mum walked in just as I tried to get another word in.

"You didn't tell us about this," said my dad, waving the letter. My mum went and stood next to him.

"We are ... well, Baljit, we are both ..."

Suddenly my mum smiled and my dad had tears in his eyes.

"We are both very proud of you, son."

I was in shock.

"You lied to us," said my mum. "That's wrong, and you know it. You should have told us."

"We never knowing it was this serious – Liverpool's coach saying you excellent player. Bright future."

"But I ... I thought you didn't want ..."

"I never want you to waste your life. This," my dad said and he waved the letter again, "this not wasting life, Baljit. This something to be very proud of. To tell you the truth, your teacher Mr Ball phone me on Saturday. I known since then."

"But why didn't you say something?"

"Couldn't surprise you then, could we?"

So that was why Mr Ball had smiled when I told him about the lie.

And then Dad came over and gave me a hug, followed by my mum. They were both in tears and so was I.

"So, I can go?" I said.

"Too right you going, beteh. You can pay for us retiring, innit." My dad grinned and picked up a tennis ball that was on the sofa. He threw it at me.

Then he grinned even wider. "Head it back, son. On me turban, innit!"

Our books are tested
for children and young people by
children and young people.

Thanks to everyone who consulted on
a manuscript for their time and effort in
helping us to make our books better
for our readers.